THE BASEBALL PLAYER'S OBSESSION

EMMA BRAY

CHAPTER
ONE

Nate

I HUFF out a breath as I meander along the sidewalk. My latest conversation with my sister is still fresh in my mind.

Is this how I made her feel all those times that I busted her balls over closing herself off and not giving any guy a chance?

I used to harp at Ella, but always with good intentions. I saw how lonely my sister secretly was, and I'm so glad that she finally gave Jesse Hamilton, the renowned basketball star, a chance.

They're married now, and all is well in paradise with a baby on the way. My sister has even talked her husband into letting her have a cat. He's not crazy about the furry felines himself, but she has him wrapped around her pretty little finger. The six-foot-six giant turns to mush in her hands.

I can't stop the grin that twitches my lips. That's exactly what I wanted for her.

And I'm happy for her, but now that Cindy has found her own happiness, she's determined to make sure I do likewise. Almost every time we talk, she tries to have a heart-to-heart with me and tell me I'm just like she was—that I shut myself off from everyone.

That's not true, though. I go on plenty of dates, and Cindy

never even dated. There's a difference.

But she is right when she points out that I never allow myself to get close to any one woman. About two weeks is a woman's shelf life in my calendar. Once the fun is over, I put her back where she came from before things can get emotional and sticky. It's not that I'm one of those asshole guys who just wants to play the field or sow his wild oats.

I know what it is. Deep down, I'm afraid of ending up like our father.

All Cindy sees when she thinks about our father is how he abandoned us. But I see the deeper picture. I see a man who loved so hard that when he lost the love of his life, it broke him.

When our mom died of cancer when we were just little kids, our dad died right along with her. He couldn't cope, so he turned to booze to black out his feelings, and in the process, he abandoned his children.

Yeah, I was bitter about it like Cindy for a while, but I can't even hate him for it anymore. Instead, I just feel a deep well of pity, and it scares me. I don't ever want to love so hard that it destroys me to lose the person. It's better off to be alone than have that happen.

Whereas Cindy wouldn't date for fear that the person would abandon her, I don't like to get attached for fear that I'll end up just like my father. Loving so hard that it wrecks me.

I scowl to myself. I don't like dwelling on this shit. I wish Cindy would just drop it.

I feel a prickle of guilt when I realize this is probably exactly how she felt when I used to nag at her, but that's different. I'm the older brother. It was my job to encourage her to take her happiness.

Cindy's issues lay within she didn't think she was good enough for anyone to stick around. Mine are more like trying to protect myself and others. It's not the same, right?

A little bell jangles overhead as I walk into the pet store where Cindy and Jesse buy their cat food. Cindy is a total psychopath about that damn cat. She will only buy this special food from this certain pet shop, and Jesse has a game tonight, but their little furball needs food.

So, here I am buying little Fluffy her food. Go figure. Looks like my sister has me wrapped around her little redheaded finger too.

Oh, well. I guess this is what big brothers are for. It's not like I was doing anything else tonight. I've already had baseball practice, and our game isn't until the weekend, so I'm free for now.

The shop is fairly empty. There's only one old lady browsing the shelves when I walk in. I don't know where the worker is. Probably in the back doing some stuff. It doesn't look like the shop is overly busy with customers right now.

I walk over to the cat food aisle and look for the special food that Cindy claims is the only food that spoiled princess cat can eat.

Jesus, if she and Jesse are like this over a damn cat, I can only imagine what they're going to be like over their child.

My eyes scan the shelves. There are so many different kinds, and I can't remember exactly what the brand my sister says it was. Kitten something or was it Fancy something?

Hell, I don't know.

"Can I help you?" a sweet,

feminine voice says from behind me.

I whirl around only to have my chest seize up like I'm having a heart attack.

I go completely still as my pulse stops and then skyrockets. I feel the blood rushing throughout my veins as I stare into a pair of midnight blue eyes. They're so blue they almost appear violet and otherworldly.

I'm looking down because this girl is impossibly short and tiny, yet she's a curvy little thing with just enough flair of hips and generous mounds for breasts to drive a man wild. Her hair is raven black and flows down her back in thick, luscious waves—all the way down to that impossibly tiny waist.

My god, she looks like some sort of little doll with her pale porcelain skin and those big midnight blue eyes framed by dark lashes. The paleness of her skin makes her little puffy pink lips appear that much brighter.

I'm staring at her, my throat tight, when her little brow furrows, and she licks her lips. My eyes home in on the motion of her pink tongue moistening her puffy flesh, and I feel myself hardening in my pants.

I bite back a groan and tear my gaze back up to her innocent-looking eyes. Fuck, this girl still looks like a teenager. I'm not old at twenty-six, but I'm probably too old to be having these thoughts about her.

I swallow, my throat working as I realize she's still waiting for an answer. "Do you work here?" I ask, sounding like the complete idiot I am. Of course, she fucking works here. She just asked me if I needed help.

Yes, I do need help, baby. I'm rendered completely immobile by you.

She smiles at me, her eyes

twinkling. "You could say that. I'm the owner."

I blink, taken aback but strangely relieved. She must be at least eighteen in order to own this joint.

She must see the surprise in my eyes because she offers softly, "My parents left it to me when they died."

I know I shouldn't pry, but I can't help myself. I want to know everything about this girl. "How did they die?"

"A car accident a few years ago," she says before she shakes her head and looks past me toward the shelves. "Looking for some cat food?"

My heart aches for her because I recognize the look of an orphan in her eyes. It's the same look me and my sister had when my mom died and then our dad left us.

I cast my eyes back over the many brands on the shelf. "Yeah, it's for my sister's cat, but I can't remember what kind she said, and apparently this cat is picky as shit and will only eat this one type of food."

The raven-haired beauty throws her head back and laughs before she asks, "What's your sister's name? If she's a regular here, I might know her and remember what she buys."

"Cindy," I tell her. Her eyes instantly light with recognition, and a smile breaks across her face as she reaches out and grabs a can of cat food and shows it to me. "This is what her kitten likes."

I take the can from her and then grab several more. "Thanks...?" I raise a questioning brow at her, prompting her for her name. My eyes have already studied her chest long enough to know she's not wearing a name badge.

"Brandy," she offers me her

name with a smile that causes my chest to ache painfully again.

"Brandy," I repeat her name, loving the way it rolls off my tongue. "I'm Nate."

She blushes as she smiles again. "Nice to meet you Nate, Cindy's brother."

My cock is a steel rod now. Hearing my name in her innocently sultry voice is almost enough to make me nut all in my jeans right here.

I follow her to the counter, admiring her ass like any red-blooded male would do. The way those jeans hug that succulent peach of an ass so perfectly….

The way those long locks sway against her back...

My fingers twitch around the cans. I'm suddenly fighting the undeniable urge to fists my hands in that hair. I have visions of me plowing into her with my hands buried in her hair, my lips smashed over her beautiful bee-stung lips, and I feel my cock aching, my balls harder than stones.

Fuck, I have never been this hard up for a woman before—especially one I just met.

"So, you're a baseball play-er," Brandy comments as she rings up the cat food.

I raise an eyebrow. "Cindy has been talking about me?"

She laughs. "Only every time she comes in here."

I roll my eyes. "No telling what she's saying about me."

"It's all good. I promise." She gives me that heart-stoppingly beautiful smile again, and it's enough to make my breath catch. Fuck, this girl is so damn beautiful.

The things she's doing to my body and chest are really fucking with my head. I want to ask her out, and I'm never shy, but the words stick in my throat. What the fuck? I've never been the guy who hesitates, but something about Brandy has me all tied up in knots.

She puts the receipt in the bag and then hands it to me. My fingers brush hers as I take it from her.

Our eyes meet as electricity snaps between us. Her eyes widen slightly, her lips parting as she stares at me.

I swallow. Fuck, does she feel it too?

She bites her lip and looks up at me from beneath those thick lashes, and all I can do is stare at the way her teeth pierce the flesh, wishing that it was me nibbling on that lip.

I finally break our staring contest before I do something crazy like lean across this counter and taste those sweet lips that are calling to me.

The old lady shuffles up behind me and claims Brandy's

attention with a warm welcome that lets me know she's a regular customer here too.

Brandy pulls her eyes away from me and smiles kindly at the old lady, effectively dismissing me.

I try to ignore the pang that causes me. When her gaze leaves mine, I feel like I've lost something precious.

I walk out of the store, my feet feeling heavier with every step I take away from her.

I stop outside and turn to look back in and admire her beautiful form as she helps the old lady with her purchases.

Something stirs inside me the longer I watch Brandy. It's something I've never felt before.

Something dark and dangerous.

Something that scares the shit out of me.

And when I try to pull myself

away from the window, my feet won't move.

My eyes are glued to her. I can't seem to look away, even though I'm trying with all my might.

I swallow hard as realization creeps over me.

I am so fucked.

CHAPTER
TWO

Brandy

MY FINGERS ARE STILL TINGLING from where Nate's brushed mine when I gave him his sister's cat food after checking him out.

And boy did I ever check him out. The man has gorgeous auburn locks and golden eyes—just like his sister. Big and tall in that way that makes women swoon.

He's a veritable god.

And good lord, the way those golden eyes burned into me like he was seeing deep inside to the heart of me, all the secret places I never let anyone see.

I told the man something I never talk about. I told him about how my parents died. Sure, I didn't go in-depth about it, but I admitted more to him than I have people who aren't complete strangers.

I still can't get over the sting of disappointment that he didn't ask me out. I'd have probably leaped into his arms like an overeager puppy, and it's not just that he's the hottest man I've ever seen in all of my nineteen years.

There's something else about him. Something I can't put my finger on. I'm drawn to him in a way I can't explain.

But none of that matters because he's gone.

I try not to let the melancholy of that thought get to me. This is crazy. I don't even really know the guy, yet I feel as depressed as if I broke up with him.

Well, what I assume people must feel like after a breakup. I wouldn't really know since I've never had a boyfriend at all before.

I know. It's pathetic, right? Most girls my age lost their v-cards years ago, and I still have my kiss card.

I've never even had a proper orgasm. I feel like an idiot because I must be doing something wrong. I've rubbed my clit just like the heroines in the naughty books I read do, but I've never been able to make myself tip over that edge.

I'm starting to think I'm defective or something.

I mean, I feel the throbbing between my legs. I feel the want, the desire, but I can't achieve that pinnacle everyone talks about.

I'm lying in my bed now, my pussy throbbing as I think of Nate. My face flushes as I feel myself getting wetter than I've ever been.

I move my hand tentatively between my legs and begin to stroke softly with memories of his golden eyes still burning in my mind.

My breathing quickens as I imagine the bulging muscles underneath his clothes. I imagine him hard down there, that *I* made him that way.

I remember the sexy gruffness of his voice. I imagine it in my ear.

Come for me, pretty baby. Come for your daddy.

I don't know where the hell that thought comes from. I never thought I was the kind of girl who was turned on by daddy kink. It never did anything for me before when I read it in books, but it causes tingles of pleasure to race along my spine when I think of Nate that way.

Nate is so big and perfect and capable, and I just know he would take care of everything.

I imagine what it would feel like to have him come in me.

"Nate!" I call out his name when this insane pressure builds in me and then pops.

Moisture gushes from between my legs, and my entire body arches up from the bed as muscles I didn't even know I had quake and spasm uncontrollably.

My eyes roll back in my head, and the last thing I imagine before I pass out is Nate's golden eyes burning down at me intensely.

————

Nate

"Motherfuck!" I grunt as my sticky seed spews up out of my spasming cock.

When I couldn't pull myself away from sweet Brandy's little pet shop, I finally decided to give over to my insanity and stalked her home.

And then I sat outside her house most of the night until I finally drug myself away to take my sister her dang cat food.

I was going insane not being able to see her inside her apartment. I have a crazy need to be able to see this girl at all times, and I know it's wrong. I know I've officially gone off the deep end, but I snuck into her house when she went to work the next day and put cameras up all over her house.

I put cameras up in her shop too.

And now all I do in between

practice is sit on my phone and stare at her. Everything she does mesmerizes me.

The way she eats. The way she chews her lip as she reads a book. The way she's not afraid of the spiders and reptiles she takes care of at the pet shop.

You would think being a pet shop owner she'd have pets of her own at home, but she doesn't. She's painfully alone.

Just like me.

My dick aches every time I look at her, and I can't even think about having a random hookup. All my cock wants is her. I'm afraid she's all it's going to want for the rest of my life.

I should just make myself known to her. Ask her out. But my obsession is already too deep, and I'm honestly afraid of what I'll do if she says no.

I might fucking snap and go off the deep end like my old man cause try as I might to not be like him, apparently I am, and all it took was one look into her midnight blue eyes to have me hooked for life.

I can't get the girl out of my head.

That's why when I see her slip her hand in between her legs, my already hard cock gets harder than the baseball bats I swing every day.

Fuuck.

There's nothing like seeing this innocent angel touch herself, and when she calls out my name when she comes on those pretty little fingers, it's like a hit of lust injected straight into my veins.

The knowledge that she was thinking of me when she got herself off makes me want to change into her bedroom, conse-quences be damned, and stuff my cock so deep inside her I'll be permanently etched into her skin.

When I finally finish busting

the biggest nut of my life, I sit there, chest heaving, contemplating my options.

I can either keep driving myself insane or go claim my girl.

Because after tonight there's no doubt about it.

Brandy Lancaster is *mine*.

CHAPTER
THREE

Brandy

MY HEART STARTS PATTERING AWAY in my chest when Nate walks into my pet shop looking sexier than sin the next morning.

My cheeks burn with the memory of how I had my first orgasm last night while thinking of him.

Apparently, all I needed all along was mental fodder like

Nate to help me climb that cliff and jump off it.

And my god went I jumped off it...

I clench my legs together now to ease the ache that's taken root deep inside me.

"Hi, Nate," I smile at him, trying my best to make my voice sound normal, but it still comes out as a breathy squeak. "What can I do for you?"

I swallow at the way his eyes smolder at me at my question.

He keeps closing the distance between us until he's standing right in front of me in all his masculine glory. My head is tipped back to look up at him, and that electric current zings through me like lightning when he takes my hands in his.

"Go out with me."

He doesn't ask it as a question. It's a demand. One that causes my core to clench with the way his voice sounds all gravelly when he says it.

I don't even hesitate or try to play coy. "When?"

He doesn't either. "Now. As soon as possible."

My heart leaps in my chest at the hungry impatience reflected in his eyes.

"The shop isn't closed yet." My voice comes out breathy.

"Aren't you the owner?" He points out before he speaks directly into my ear. "Close this place up, princess, and come with me before I go insane."

I tremble both at the way he calls me "princess" and the way his hot breath fans over the shell of my ear.

"Okay," I whisper before I do as he says with shaky hands. I feel his eyes on me the entire time.

When I've finally got everything locked up, Nate is there waiting for me with an outstretched hand, looking like a dream come true. I have to resist the urge to pinch myself and make sure I'm not still dreaming.

I dreamt of him all night after that first cataclysmic orgasm.

When his big hand closes around mine, a feeling of safety like I've never known falls over me, and I know in this moment I would trust this man with my life.

I don't even ask where he's taking me.

I'll follow him anywhere.

Nate

I can't believe this beautiful woman is sitting across from me, letting me hold her hand while we have dinner together. Everything about her is perfect. I can't take my eyes off of her.

I devour every inch of her face. She's got a smoking hot body too, no doubt, but it's her face that I love more than anything.

Those beautiful midnight blue eyes, those long, raven tresses, the sound of her pretty little voice. I never thought I had a kink, but if I do, it's definitely the sound of Brandy's voice. It's sweet and innocent, yet sultry and sexy at the same time.

I could listen to her talk all day about absolutely anything. I don't taste the food. I don't even pay attention to what I order. I just tell the waiter to bring me the same thing that my girl is having.

It's unbelievable, but she seems to be into me too. I love the way her cheeks flush at every touch. For once, I don't mind answering a girl's questions.

"Ask me anything you want, baby. I'll tell you anything you want to know."

And I mean it too. I'm an open book for her. Nothing is off-limits for my Brandy.

I realize this is insane for someone who was so dead set against falling in love just a few days ago, but this is as unstoppable as a freight train. There's no slowing it down.

There's no stopping the way I feel. I was a fool to think I could ever try. One look at Brandy is all it took for me to fall so deep down the rabbit hole that I'll never be able to dig my way out —and I don't even want to.

I'm still terrified she's going to destroy me, but it'll be worth it. She can do whatever she wants to me.

What I'm more terrified of now is hurting her. I don't want to have any secrets from her, but there is one big one looming over my head, and that's the way I've been stalking her.

How am I ever supposed to tell her that? Something tells me she's not going to be okay with that. She keeps looking at me with those dreamy violet eyes.

"I didn't know guys like you existed," she admits in a husky little murmur that sends my pulse racing and causes guilt to clog my insides. She thinks I'm her prince charming, and God, do I want to be, but I feel more like the evil villain with my deceit.

I push all of that out of my mind for the time being, though. I'm not going to waste the precious moments I have with her stressing over something I can't change. I'll deal with that when the time comes.

I will tell her eventually—when the time is right. Surely, she'll understand what she and I have. I just can't help it. My obsession with her runs deeper than anything I've ever experienced before.

We finish our dinner, and panic lights in my chest at the thought of taking her home. I can't let her go now.

"Come back with me to my place." I say it is a demand but try to make my voice pose it as a question. I want her to feel like she has a choice, even though I don't know if I'll be able to let her go if she says no.

Her cheeks turn a beautiful shade of pink before she licks her lips and nods shyly. "Okay."

My cock is a steel rod in my pants as I take her hand and lead her to my car. I wonder if that shade of pink on her cheeks matches the pink of what I already know is going to be the prettiest little pussy in the entire world.

I feel her fingers trembling in mine, and I bring them up to my lips and kiss them gently, wordlessly assuring her that everything's going to be okay. I keep my eyes pinned on her the entire time, trying to convey to her just how much I adore her. How much I want to worship every inch of her body.

How I don't just want to fuck her. I want to make love to her. Not just her body either. I want to make love to her mind, her soul. I want to wrap myself so tightly around her that the world dissolves into nothing but her and me.

My cock is leaking and making a mess of my boxers, but fuck if I can make it go down. Being this close to brandy does something to me I can't control. It's something primal. Some instinct that I can't deny.

An instinct that's telling me to claim her once and for all as mine and only mine.

Brandy

THE PROMISES SMOLDERING in Nate's golden eyes have my heart beating a mile a minute. It's like the air around us is charged with energy.

We don't speak much on the ride to his place, but Nate touches me at all times. He drives with a hand on my knee or with his hand clasped over mine, and it's like I'm feeding off of his touch. I feel the warmth flowing from him into me.

It's the most spiritual thing I've ever felt before. Our connection is a live thing pulsing between us, and every time I peek glances over at him, my heart jumps up into my throat.

He finally pulls his hand away from mine to turn into his driveway, but his hands aren't off me for long because no sooner does he kill the engine than he's out of the car and coming around to the passenger side to pull me out.

He wraps his arms around my waist as he pulls me up, and then we stare at each other, both of our breath catching as our eyes collide.

I can't tell who makes the first move, but suddenly, our lips are pressed together.

I instantly open for him. His

tongue slides into my mouth, and dear lord, the way this man kisses me…

He kisses me like he's dying and I'm the only thing that can save him. He kisses me like he's staking a claim and damn but I *want* to be claimed by him.

This is the stuff romance novels are made of—the way his big arm circles around me and lifts me…the way my legs instinctively wrap around his waist.

We both thread our fingers into each other's hair. Nate angles my head the way he wants to deepen the kiss, stroking the flame within me higher and higher.

I'm gone. I can't think of anything but the insistent pressure of his lips on mine and the way the huge bulge in his pants is pressing right against my engorged clit.

I don't even think about it before I start humping against him, sliding my mound up and down his rigid length.

Stars burst behind my closed eyes, and he groans into my mouth as he pushes back into me. My eyes flutter open, and I barely get a glimpse of his house before we become a tangle of limbs. It's a good thing Nate's house is a bit off the road because here we are standing outside, dry-humping each other like animals in heat.

Even though my entire body is flushed, it's not from embar-rassment. It's from hunger and just what this man does to me. He could pull my pants down and take me right here and I wouldn't utter a word of protest.

But it seems Nate is able to keep a clearer head than me because the next thing I know, I feel my back hit a wall. I open my eyes again to see that he's carried me indoors.

My breath hitches when I see his golden orbs burning down into me before he claims my lips again.

I close my eyes and whimper, kissing him back.

"Fuck, princess, do you know what you do to me? You're driving me fucking wild."

Before I can say anything, he kisses me again, and then he trails those kisses all along my jawline and over the column of my throat.

I don't know what it is about him kissing my throat, but it sends wetness pooling between my thighs.

"Nate," I whimper his name, and it's like I've pressed a turbo button on the man. He suddenly pulls me from the wall and carries me through his house before he falls onto the bed with me.

He carefully cradles my body and keeps himself from putting his entire weight on top of me as we crash, our lips colliding again as I dry hump against him furiously, shamelessly. I should be embarrassed, but I can't control myself.

"Goddamn, baby. You keep this up you're going to be the death of me, you know that?" he growls as he slips my shirt over my head and pulls down my pants.

I struggle to pull his shirt off him. He helps me, and grabs it, tugging it off with one arm in that super sexy way only guys can do.

I try not to pant like a bitch in heat as I ogle the muscles lining his chest and abdomen. The man is sex on a stick—seriously.

And when he slips down his boxers and pants in one fluid movement, his huge erection bobs free. My eyes widen when I see the moisture beading the tip and take in the sheer length and girth of him.

He spreads my legs wide, his gaze pinned at the sensitive flesh between them. My cheeks are burning, but I don't even try to cover myself. I'm modest and self-conscious as hell, but the way his eyes are drinking me up gives me courage. I let him look his fill, and when a guttural groan tears up out of his chest as he falls to his knees in front of me, it's like a balm to my soul.

"Just look at this pretty little thing. Got to get a taste of it," he murmurs almost reverently.

And then his mouth is on me. He laves me with one possessive lick from slit to clit before he starts to suck and slurp on me in earnest.

It's filthy the noises he's making, but they're turning me

on like nothing else. He's groaning and growling as he goes down on me, and it only causes me to spasm more when I look down and see him fisting his huge cock and stroking it up and down while he feasts on me.

"That's right, baby," he encourages me as his golden eyes capture mine. "I felt that little spasm. Keep going, princess. Come all over your daddy's tongue."

I don't know what it is about that word, but it sends such a shockwave running through me. I remember how I came thinking of Nate calling himself my daddy before and now here he is doing it in the flesh. It's all I need to send me tipping over the edge.

And holy moly, this orgasm is ten times more intense than the first one I gave myself. I'm screaming, fisting my hands in Nate's hair. He holds my legs open as I shake and spasm underneath him.

"Yes, that's it," he hisses against my flesh in between licks. "Give it all to me. Mine. All mine. Every drop of you."

I feel like I've exited my body. I'm floating above it all, and when I finally come back to, Nate is hovering over me, his thick rod prodding at my entrance. I'm so wet he slips easily in until he hits my virgin barrier.

His eyes widen when he feels the resistance, and I tense. His mouth falls open as he looks down at me in wonder as he cautiously probes against it again before pulling back.

"Brandy," his voice sounds strangled, "are you a virgin?"

My cheeks flame as I bite my lip and nod.

"Fuck," he groans, every muscle in his body shaking as he tries to hold back. "Princess, are you sure—?" he starts to ask me, but I am so close to having the man of my dreams I don't even wait for him to finish the question.

I wrap my legs around him and pull on his ass while I thrust my hips up at him, plunging myself down onto him and breaking the barrier of my virginity.

I gasp out at the sting and the sudden fullness inside me.

"Fuck!" Nate roars out as he slides into me.

He's still not all the way in, though. He pulls his cock out and pushes it back in several times, feeding me more inches each time. God, the man is so big. Is he ever going to bottom out inside me?

I'm panting and clinging to him by the time he finally gets himself all the way inside me. Oh god, I feel the head of his cock kissing my cervix, and I clench around him involuntarily.

Nate is going crazy. He buries his face in my neck as he growls out, "Fuck, look at you, princess, taking all of Daddy's inches so good. Such a good girl, aren't you? You're going to let Daddy ride this pussy, aren't you, baby? You're going to let me nut in you bareback, aren't you?"

My pussy clenches harder at every filthy word he says until I hear myself moaning, "Yes! Yes!"

He spears his hands in my hair as he hammers his long rod in and out of me, each stroke sending me higher and higher. "You want Daddy to breed you, don't you? You want me to flood this little pussy with my seed until you swell with my child?"

This is insane for him to be talking like this, but fuck if his possessive, caveman words aren't turning me on.

"Yes!" I call out, never meaning anything more.

"Fuck, Brandy!" He growls out my name just as I clamp down hard on him, my orgasm ripping through me like a tidal wave.

His heat floods me, and I feel his cock jerking inside me. He's still jerking inside me, releasing his hot seed into my belly while my pussy flutters around him when he grabs my face, his eyes boring down into mine. "Mine," he whispers ardently before he claims my lips voraciously. "This is more than just sex, Brandy, you know that right?" His lips slide against mine with every impassioned word he speaks. "You're mine now. Every bit of you. I'm your daddy from this moment on, and I'm never going to let you go. I'm going to take such good care of you. I swear to you, princess."

His words burrow straight

into my heart, and I'm overcome with emotion. I bury my head into his neck and nod.

Yes, I want that too. I am his. I always want to be his. Now and forever.

Brandy

NATE DOESN'T LET me out of his sight for the next week. When he goes to practice, he drags me along with him and sits me on the sidelines where he can look over at me. He glances over at me all the time as if to make sure I'm still there.

When I open my shop, he's right there with me, sitting behind the counter or helping out with the stocking in the back.

We shower together. We eat together. We sleep together. We do everything together. Sometimes we stay at his place. Sometimes we stay at my place. Wherever we are, we're always together. His hand is always on some part of me. Either that or he's completely buried inside me. If we're not joined physically, we might as well be because he's so deep inside my heart now they would have to cut me completely open to dig him out.

Everything is perfect, and I can't imagine how anything could ever come between us.

Until one day it does.

Nate is in the bathroom after one of our intense lovemaking sessions. I stretch leisurely in the bed like a contented feline, a goofy smile on my face at the way he just ravished me.

My phone buzzes on the nightstand, and I pick it up to

check the notification, but when I get the phone in my hand, I realize it's not my phone.

I'm not one of those girls who feels the need to snoop on her man, but when I start to put it down, something catches my attention on the screen.

My eyes widen when I realize I'm looking at a video feed of my house, and the notification on it was showing where the bug guy showed up to spray. I left a key out so he could get in since I knew I wouldn't be there tonight since I'm staying over with Nate.

My heart starts hammering away in my chest when the gravity of what I'm seeing settles over me.

Nate has cameras in my apartment. How did he get cameras in my apartment? *Why* does he have cameras in my apartment? How long has he had cameras in my apartment?

All I can do is stare at the

screen, dumbfounded as I imagine all the things Nate has seen me do.

When he walks out of the bathroom, he goes completely still as he sees me holding his phone in my hand.

"Nate," my voice comes out shaky as I hold up the phone and show him the screen. "What is this?"

One look into his eyes is like a stab straight to my heart.

The guilt is written all over his face. Betrayal twists my gut. I leap up from the bed. I don't know what I'm thinking. I'm just following some instinct that tells me to run, but Nate circles around the bed quick as a flash and grabs me from behind, pulling my back flush against his chest.

"It's not what you think, Brandy. Well, then what the fuck is it, Nate, because it looks like you've been spying on me."

Nate's arms band tighter around me before he turns me to face him and holds me still with his hands on my shoulders.

I struggle in his grasp, but he refuses to release me. "I'm not some crazy stalker, Brandy. I know what it might look like, but I swear I'm not. It's just that from the moment I first set eyes on you I couldn't tear myself away from you. I became obsessed with you, and it's something I swore I would never do. You know I didn't want to end up like my father."

I soften. I remember Nate telling me about how his dad completely lost it when his mom died. That's why Nate always held himself back from love.

But he's never held himself back from me.

"One look at you, Brandy," he goes on, "and I just couldn't do it. I couldn't pretend that I wasn't completely in love with you. Yeah, I know. It might be the cheesy shit that rom-coms are made of, but it was love at first sight. When I saw you, I just knew you were meant to be mine, but I was too scared to approach you. I was too afraid of how deep my obsession with you already was, but it was killing me to not be able to see you every moment of the day.

"So, I did the only thing I could do, and I might be wrong, Brandy, but I'm not sorry. I'm not going to lie to you. I'd do it all over again. You know I love you. You know that's real. And if you think there's any way in hell I'll let you walk out the door, you're the one who's crazy, baby, because I don't give a fuck if I have to kidnap you and chain you to me at this point. You're not going anywhere, princess."

His eyes are wild, and his chest is heaving at the end of his monologue.

I stare at him in shock as I try to process everything he's just told me. I don't even know how to feel about it.

I know what I should be feeling, and that's fear. So then why do I feel a little flutter of pleasure in my belly?

It's because I'm sick. I'm sick too because deep down a part of me *likes* that he's so obsessed with me like this.

That he would go to such extreme lengths to have me. I don't know what my expression is telling him, but it's something that causes panic to flash over his face.

"Brandy," his voice breaks. "It would completely wreck me to lose you."

He falls down on his knees and wraps his arms around my hips, pressing the side of his face against my stomach.

His shoulders shake, and I realize he's crying. Something

about seeing this big, capable man on his knees sobbing before me has me sliding to my knees too.

Tears stream down my own cheeks as I take his face in my hands and find his golden gaze that I love so much.

"I felt it too," I tell him. A feeling of serenity passes over me. It doesn't matter. That first day we met, I felt that electric spark too.

Nate's eyes are so vulnerable as he gathers me close to him and buries his face in my neck.

"I'm yours, Nate," I tell him as I cradle his head against me and run my fingers through his hair soothingly.

He begins to kiss all over the side of my neck, moving his kisses up until he's kissing all over my cheeks, my forehead, and then finally my lips.

"Brandy, my precious angel, I'd do anything for you.

Anything but let you go. You understand that, don't you?"

I look into his golden eyes and nod, my heart swelling. Yes, I do understand, but I can't form the words. Instead, I kiss Nate, communicating to him everything I feel, sealing my promise with a kiss.

Nate's arms band around me possessively—almost painfully—as he kisses me back hungrily.

"Mine," he rasps against my hair.

I don't care if it's a little fucked up.

Stalker or not, I am Nate's.

Now and forever.

EPILOGUE

Nate

Three Months Later

THE CROWD GOES wild as I hit the last home run that wins us the game, but all I care about and all I can see is my beautiful girl standing on the sidelines.

My eyes pass over her gently swollen belly. I swear there's nothing more erotic than seeing my woman pregnant with our unborn child.

Like I do after every game, I hoist her in my arms. Her arms and legs wrap around my waist, and I kiss her right there on the field in front of everyone. It's kind of become our tradition, and the crowd loves it, which is a good thing because I wouldn't give a fuck if they didn't. Nothing could ever keep me from my Brandy.

When I finally pull back and allow us to catch our breath, she beams at me, her beautiful raven locks hanging down behind her.

Her midnight blue eyes twinkle up at me. "You hit another home run."

My chest swells at the pride in her voice.

"I did," I agree, "but now I'm trying to see how many bases I can get to with my wife."

She blushes prettily before she whispers in my ear, "Take me home, and maybe you'll hit another home run."

That's all the encouragement I need, but fuck if I'm going to wait until we get home. My cock is about to bust out of my pants as it is.

"And what if I can't make it that long?" I whisper back to her.

She bites her lip, and I already know my answer.

I carry her into the locker room and find an empty room to lock us up in. It's scarcely more than a broom closet. There's barely enough room for two people, but we're not going to be two people for very long.

I already have her dress hiked up. She fumbles with my pants until I hurriedly free my aching cock.

She's so ready that one thrust is all it takes for me to completely seat myself inside her.

"Fuck!" I groan out as her hot heat engulfs me. My balls are harder than the baseballs I hit all day long, and she's so tight and hot that all it takes is a couple of pumps before I feel my seed boiling.

"Fuck, Brandy, how do you do this to me?" I keep thinking my endurance will get better over time, but it's just the opposite. I seem to come faster every time with her.

I feel the first fluttering of her around me and groan. "Are you going to come for Daddy, princess?" I growl in her ear, knowing exactly what will set her off.

Just like clockwork, she detonates when she hears me call myself her daddy.

"Daddy!" she screams as her pussy clenches down on me so hard I see stars.

"Fuck!" I roar as my seed tears up out of my balls. I feel it shooting up my stalk before it burst through the tip, and I start pumping it into her violently.

I hold myself deep. Even though she's already pregnant, I'm trying to spray every bit of myself inside her like I'm still trying to knock her up. I can't help it. That's my instinct with her. Claim. Breed. *Mine.*

She goes limp in my arms before I tilt her head up to kiss her sweet lips. "I fall more and more in love with you every day," I tell her.

She smiles at me, those gorgeous eyes of hers softening as she strokes my cheek tenderly. "I love you, Nate."

Those words make my soul sing and get my blood pumping faster than any high-stakes baseball game. I hit a home run, all right.

When I scored Brandy. My princess. My everything.

Want more Emma Bray? Sign up
to my newsletter to get a free
book: www.
authoremmabray.com.

www.ingramcontent.com/pod-product-compliance
Lightning Source LLC
Chambersburg PA
CBHW021347160726
47994CB00007B/2867